This book
belongs to

....

p

Pirates

Written by Nick Ellsworth, Caroline Repchuk,
Geoff Cowan, Claire Keen, Kat Wooton
Illustrated by Anna Leplar (Elizabeth Roy Literary Agency),
Robin Edmonds, Chris Forsey, Diana Catchpole
Design by Mike Hodgson, Dirty Cat Co.

This is a Parragon Publishing book
This edition published in 2006

Parragon Publishing
Queen Street House
4 Queen Street
Bath
BA1 1HE, UK

Printed in China

ISBN 1-40547-072-0

Contents

Buried Treasure

Jim lived in an old house with a rambling garden. The house was spooky, but Jim liked the garden. He spent hours playing ball and climbing the trees. It was a wonderful garden to play in, but Jim was lonely. How he wished he had someone to play with! He had plenty of friends at school, but his school friends found

his house so spooky that they only came to visit once.

One day Jim was playing in the garden with a stick. As he was poking about under some leaves he saw a piece of metal sticking out of the ground. He reached down and pulled it free. In his hand lay a rusty old key.

Jim carried the key indoors and cleaned it. Then he set about trying to find the lock that it fitted. First he tried the old garden gate that had been locked as long as Jim could remember. But the key was far too small. Next he tried the grandfather clock in the hall, but this time it was too big.

Then Jim had an idea. "Perhaps the key fits something in the attic," he thought. He was usually too scared to go into the attic. But now he was so determined to find the key's home that he ran up the stairs boldly and opened the door. He caught sight of a large book sticking out from one of the shelves. It was fitted with a lock. Jim lifted down the book and put it on the floor.

His fingers trembled as he put the key in the lock. It fitted perfectly! Jim slowly opened the book and turned the pages.

Suddenly, he heard a voice coming from the book! "You have unlocked my secrets," it said.

"Step into my pages if you are looking for adventure."

Jim found himself stepping onto the book.

As he put his foot on the pages he found he was falling. The next thing he knew he was on the deck of a ship. He looked up and saw a tattered flag with a skull and crossbones on it.

He was on a pirate ship!

Just then, Jim saw that all the pirates were jumping overboard and swimming to the shore. Jim swam, too.

When he reached the shore he found he was on
a desert island! The pirates went searching for something
to make a shelter. Just then, one of them came running
toward him waving a knife. "You thief, you stole my
rubies!" cursed the pirate in a menacing voice.

What was Jim to do?
Then he heard a voice calling from the book,
"Quick! Step back here!"

Jim stepped into the book and suddenly he was
back in the attic again.

Jim peered closely at the page from which he'd just stepped. "The Pirates and the Stolen Treasure" it said at the top of the page. Jim found he was reading exactly the adventure he had been in.

He was thrilled! He realized that he could open the book at any page and become part of the adventure, and he only had to find the book and step into it to get back to the attic again.

After that, Jim had many more adventures, and he was never lonely again!

The Pirate's Hat

Each summer, Patrick used to stay with his Uncle Max and Auntie Jess, who lived by the sea.

One afternoon, Patrick was bored. Looking around, he found a book about pirates. He read all about a pirate called One-Armed Jake. "I'm glad I'll never meet him," thought Patrick. "He's really scary!"

The next day was warm and sunny, and Patrick couldn't wait to go outdoors. He made his way down the steep path to the beach.

Suddenly, he spotted the entrance to a small cave.

"It's very dark in here," thought Patrick, as he stepped inside the cave. Then he saw something in the sand. He picked it up, and was amazed to see that it was an old pirate's hat. "Wow!" cried Patrick, putting it on his head.

Suddenly, he felt very tired. He lay down on the floor and fell asleep. When he woke up, Patrick realized that he was no longer in the cave. He was on the deck of a ship—in the middle of a battle!

All around him, pirates were fighting with swords! Suddenly, Patrick found himself staring into the eyes of a pirate with one arm. "It's One-Armed Jake!" thought Patrick with horror.

Bobbing around in a row boat in the sea below were two more pirates. Between them was a wooden chest.

"Get in the row boat, lad," snarled One-Armed Jake. He pushed Patrick into the waiting boat.

"Row, me shipmates, row!" yelled One-Armed Jake. "We're going to the beach to bury my money. My old enemy, Cap'n Saltwater, wants to steal it from me."

One-Armed Jake opened the box, and Patrick saw hundreds of gold coins inside. He noticed that a single gold coin had fallen to the bottom of the boat.

He put it in his pocket.

When they arrived at the beach, they buried the treasure chest.

"Cap'n Saltwater won't get my treasure now!" laughed One-Armed Jake.

"But the boy knows where the treasure's hidden!" growled one pirate, "He could come back and steal it!"

"That's true," said One-Armed Jake, "Maybe we should bury him with the treasure. Anyway," he roared, "the boy's got my favorite hat!" and he grabbed it off Patrick's head.

At that moment, there was a huge flash, and suddenly the pirates disappeared! Patrick was lying alone in the cave. He sat up and rubbed his eyes.

"What a scary dream," he thought.

Patrick ran back to the cottage to tell his Uncle Max and Auntie Jess what had happened.

"How terrifying! I'm glad it was just a dream," said Uncle Max, after listening to Patrick's story. Then, all of a sudden, something fell out of Patrick's pocket. When they saw what it was, they all gasped with surprise.

There on the floor lay a shiny, bright gold coin.

21

Fiddlefingers

Captain Brassbuttons hummed happily and tapped his feet to a lively tune on board his pirate ship, The Jolly Jig. Around him other pirates played tambourines and accordions.

"Look lively, lads! Ha-ha-ha!" bellowed Captain Brassbuttons, who was really enjoying himself. So were his band of buccaneers. You see, these pirates preferred making music to raiding ships and

carrying off their treasure—for The Jolly Jig was a ghost ship and Captain Brassbuttons and his crew were ghost pirates!

"'Tis a pity we don't have a fiddle player among us, cap'n," said Patch one day, as he rested against the ship's wheel.

"To be sure!" sighed Brassbuttons. "That would be more of a treasure than all the booty we've ever bagged! Now, tis high time we made ready to set sail again!"

"Aye, aye, cap'n!" said Patch.

A short while later, The Jolly Jig rose majestically from beneath the waves to haunt the high seas. Passengers on passing ships would stare in amazement at the sight

of the phantom ship. From its glowing decks came the sound of music and merry voices, as the creepy crew sang and played. That night, as The Jolly Jig sank again toward its watery grave, the crew were surprised to see that the wreck of another old vessel lay in the soft sand nearby.

"Ahoy, me hearties!" Brassbuttons called his men and pointed eagerly. "'Tis time to go a-pirating again!" And before long the pirate raiding party set off in their longboat toward the wreck.

"Stand by to board," growled Brassbuttons, leading his sea spooks on to the ship. There was a terrible noise coming from a dark corner which made him tremble.

"Who goes there?" he called, trying to sound fearless. Then he saw that the noise was coming from a phantom figure lying asleep in a hammock. To Brassbuttons' surprise, he saw there was a fiddle resting on the sailor's chest. Brassbuttons poked him with his cutlass and the sailor woke with a start.

"Who are you?" asked Captain Brassbuttons.

"The crew called me Fiddlefingers, seeing as I was always playing this fiddle," said the sailor. "I've been stuck here, all alone. The others abandoned ship before it sank! But I was playing my fiddle at the time and didn't hear their warning!"

"A fiddle-player, you say? Then 'tis good fortune we found you!" boomed Brassbuttons. However, he soon changed his mind. For instead of the tuneful harmony they had hoped to hear, he made a fearful, scratching screech. So that day spelled doom for the sorry spooks aboard The Jolly Jig. There was no more laughter, dancing, or merry music, only the woeful wails of the poor suffering crew, as they tried to drown out the sound of the awful fiddling. As for Fiddlefingers, he just smiled happily and played on, and on, and on...